This book belongs to:

_____

_____

_____

First published 2014 by Walker Books Ltd
87 Vauxhall Walk, London SE11 5HJ

This edition published 2017

2 4 6 8 10 9 7 5 3 1

© 1990 – 2017 Lucy Cousins
Lucy Cousins font © 1990 – 2017 Lucy Cousins

Illustrated in the style of Lucy Cousins by King Rollo Films Ltd

Maisy™. Maisy is a trademark of Walker Books Ltd, London.

The right of Lucy Cousins to be identified as author/illustrator of this work
has been asserted by her in accordance with the Copyright,
Designs and Patents Act 1988.

Printed in China

British Library Cataloguing in Publication Data:
a catalogue record for this book is
available from the British Library.

ISBN 978-1-4063-8300-3

www.walker.co.uk

Maisy Plays Football

Lucy Cousins

WALKER BOOKS
AND SUBSIDIARIES
LONDON • BOSTON • SYDNEY • AUCKLAND

Good morning, Maisy! What an exciting day! Maisy is going to play football. And all her friends are playing, too.

Maisy gets dressed in her special football kit. She ties the laces on her boots. Don't forget the ball, Maisy!

Hello everyone! Dotty, Tallulah and Charley are on the blue team.

"Let's warm up!"

Maisy, Cyril and Eddie are on the red team.

"Go Team!"

It's time to start. The referee blows his whistle – WHEE!

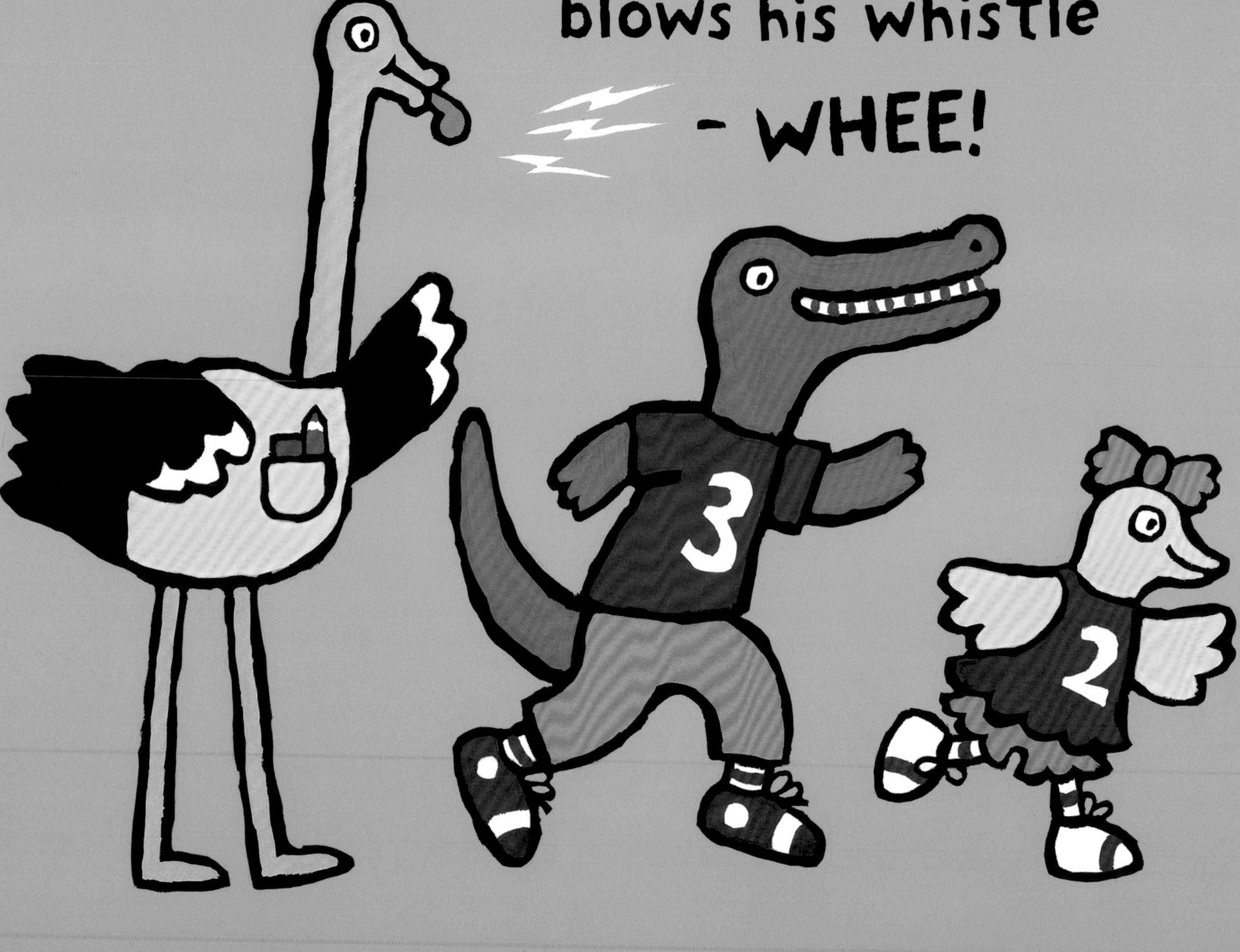

Maisy is the first to kick
the ball...

FOUMPHHH!
Up it goes!

Up, UP and ...
over Cyril's head!

Now Charley
has the ball!

He passes it
to Tallulah...

Tallulah runs fast and kicks the ball - **BOUF!**

"Yippee for the Reds!"

"Whoo! Come on the Blues!"

Right into the goal.

Hooray! The blue team have scored a goal.

It's half time!

Everyone is really thirsty from all that running around. They eat some juicy oranges.

What an exciting game! Cyril passes to Maisy,

Maisy zig-zags around Charley,

Talullah tries
to tackle ...

but Maisy
kicks it
to Cyril.

Wow, Cyril's so fast!
He really wants to score
a goal for the red team.
Come on, Cyril!
You can do it!

He runs and runs and gives the ball one BIG kick into the net ...
GOOOOOOAL!

WHEEEEEE! The referee blows his whistle. It's time to finish.

One goal for the red team, and
one goal for the blue team.
Well done everybody!

"It's a draw!"

Maisy and her friends love playing football. It doesn't matter who wins, it's just so much fun.

Maisy

Friends • Learning • Fun

- **Join Maisy and all her friends on the football pitch!**
- **Kicking and passing, diving and scoring – what a game!**
- **Perfect for children 3 years +**

Collect all the Maisy First Experiences Books:

Maisy Goes to the Library • Maisy Goes to the Museum • Maisy Goes to Hospital
Maisy Goes to Nursery • Maisy Goes on Holiday • Maisy Goes to the City • Maisy Goes on a Sleepover
Maisy Goes Camping • Maisy Learns to Swim • Maisy Goes to the Cinema • Maisy Goes by Plane
Maisy's Sports Day • Maisy Goes to the Bookshop • Maisy Goes to a Wedding • Maisy Goes to a Show
Maisy Gets a Pet • Maisy's Chinese New Year • Maisy's Surprise Birthday Party • Maisy's Snowy Day
Maisy Goes on a Nature Walk • Maisy Goes to the Dentist

www.maisyfun.com

FSC
www.fsc.org
MIX
Paper | Supporting
responsible forestry
FSC® C008047

ISBN 978-1-4063-8300-3

£6.99
UK ONLY

9 781406 383003

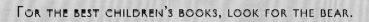

FOR THE BEST CHILDREN'S BOOKS, LOOK FOR THE BEAR.